Jack

Alex Westhaven

Jack
ISBN 978-1-937477-34-9
Copyright © 2013 Alex Westhaven
Published by Brazen Snake Books
All rights reserved.

Also by the Author

Angel Eyes

Sprouted

Lettuce Prey

No Hazard Pay

Jack

Orange flesh splattered wide as the small pumpkin hit the wall, errant strings landing on a tall metal shelving unit. Brad slumped back in the folding chair with a heavy sigh.

"This isn't working," he said, surveying the room.

Flat seeds and fibrous yellow chunks littered every flat surface of the garage, including the newspaper covered six foot table where two pumpkins still sat miraculously intact. Each attempt to carve the perfect face for this year's neighborhood "Jack" jack-o-lantern contest had tested his patience closer to the breaking point, until finally he'd found some small measure of satisfaction in smashing every single one against the concrete walls.

Every year he lost. Every year the jackass down the block got all creative and came up with something so unique that Brad's pumpkins looked positively childish, despite the fact that he'd turned forty several years ago. It didn't matter that the same guy beat everyone else as well - none of them deserved to win anyway. No one put as much time and effort into perfect pumpkin carving than Brad Nelson.

This year would be different. Brad was determined to show everyone that he was the best. His Jack would scare everyone right out of their pathetic little costumes. The thought of them screaming in fear and running back down the walk brought a smile to his lips.

But first, he had to come up with the perfect design, and so far, none of his ideas had worked. He needed inspiration. A starting point.

Pushing up out of the chair, he patted his pocket to make sure his keys were there and slipped out the side door to the driveway where his sedate black sedan waited. Brad sent a friendly wave and smile to the Kelly kids, a quick stare and intentional snub to the annoyingly loud Carson woman across the street, and a quick nod to the new neighbor on the other side mowing his lawn. Social niceties out of the way, he slid behind the wheel and just barely restrained himself from hitting the idiotic florescent fake kid in the street that demanded he slow down due to the short human population.

Whatever.

Nearing his favorite bar, Brad considered a drink, but reminded himself that Halloween was in a week so focus was necessary. Instead, he went to the mall and parked, taking a long, deep breath before he dared to venture out. If anything could inspire him, it would be here. A conversation, an expression, maybe even a store display. He just knew he needed to get out and see, hear, feel.

Brad had a good feeling as he locked the car and hiked toward the nearest doors, keeping his eyes and ears open. This was it. Today was the day. This year, his Jack was gonna shine, no matter what he had to do to make it happen.

* * * *

Wandering through the mall, Brad peered at all the window displays, watching the teens chat and laugh and text as he moseyed past the shops. Disappointingly, there wasn't much in the way of Halloween decor, and even the yellows and golds of autumn were fast being pushed aside by the coming wave of red and green and white. A few stores dared toward the dark though, and one playing loud rock music and sporting a spinning disco ball inside the dim interior caught his attention.

A skeleton in a top hat grinned down from the upper regions of the window, bony arms spread wide with black cloth wings attached at the shoulders. Various candles and lanterns flickered from cloth-covered pillars, and sitting in front of those, jack-olanterns grinned, scowled and leered as he leaned in for a closer look.

One in particular stood out, and his brows furrowed in the window's reflection as he knelt down to look the jack in the eye. He wasn't sure if it was a jawbreaker or gummy candy, but the eye looked real enough with bloodshot veins and a dripped coating of some red syrup underneath. Candy corn teeth and some sort of waxy ears gave the jack a sweetly sinister appearance, and with a little extra gorification...

Rising to his feet, Brad smiled. Inspired, he went inside and purchased a few things, and then stopped at the local Halloween store for a few more. His purchases tucked in the back seat, he made one last stop at the pumpkin patch on main street and then headed for home, feeling more optimistic than he had in days.

As he turned the car onto his street, he noticed Mason's garage door open. Driving slowly, he turned his head to look as he passed, nearly stopping with a guttural sound as he got a better look at the pumpkin sitting in the center of Mason's table.

Fucking gummy eyeballs stared back at him as he went past. He should have known.

Pulling into his driveway, he cut the engine and sat staring at his own garage door. Mason couldn't win. It was his turn. He deserved to win, damn it! There had to be something he could do that would upstage even the candy face. Dremel carving had already been done. Celebrity faces, monsters, stick-ins and stick-ons. Hell the only thing they hadn't done was...

His lips curved up. Pressing the button to open the door, Brad got out of the car and carefully unloaded his packages and pumpkins. There were five in all, four would be practice and used along the walk, the fifth would be his perfect Jack, completed on Halloween day.

Rubbing his hands together, he pushed the button to close the garage and went into the house to make dinner. This year's Jack would be the greatest masterpiece ever, and the entire neighborhood would be terrified.

Especially Mason.

* * * *

The next day, Brad cleaned the garage. There would be no more throwing pumpkins against the wall - with only five days to Halloween, there was no time for temper tantrums. He had a plan.

Tossing the last bag into the dumpster out back, he waved at the neighbor across the alley and went back to the garage. Spreading out newspapers across the length of the now-clear table, he placed a pumpkin in the center, along with the first of the sketches he'd drawn last night. With the care of a surgeon he laid out his tools on a towel to the left, and the other various items he'd need to the right. Finally, he adjusted his padded stool to the perfect height for the perspective required, and sat for twenty minutes, examining the bright squash with a critical eye on all sides.

It was time to begin.

He worked slowly. Methodically. Each line cut, burned, or shaped until it was exactly right. The room grew darker, finally lit only by the single bulb overhead, but still he worked on. It was hours before he pushed back from the table to survey his first practice piece, back aching and fingers sore and stiff.

He examined it from all angles, took some pictures, made some notes, checked again, and made more notes. When he was done, he wrapped the pumpkin and placed it in the empty refrigerator to hold until Halloween.

Four more days. Taking his notes, he went inside and heated up a frozen dinner.

Pouring over the notes and photos later, he thought perhaps the eye sockets were too far apart, but ketchup thinned with water seemed like a good choice for blood. The eyes would move in the final version, of course, but as far as prototypes went, he thought it was pretty good.

Setting the notes aside, he finished off the last of whatever that reheated mess had been and tossed the container in the trash. Popping the top on another bottle of beer, he checked the clock and went out to the front porch to settle on the swing.

Five minutes later, May Walker came up the front steps, right on time.

"Hey there, handsome. Lookin' for a little action tonight?" She smiled, her firm, faux breasts straining the low-scalloped neckline of her too-tight tee. Brad nodded, not even bothering to look at her face. Any woman showing that much cleavage clearly wanted the attention down there, he figured. She hadn't complained yet.

"I sure do May," he said, licking his lips at the taut peaks poking at the thin fabric barely covering them. "I was wondering," he said, finally looking her in the eye. "Can we try something a little different tonight? I'm in a bit of a creative mood this week, what with the Jack contest and all."

She glanced over her shoulder, making sure no one was around and then pulled her shirt down to expose those glorious globes.

"Anything you want, sugar. Just tell me what to do."

He stood up and grabbed her wrist, pulling her toward the garage as he tried to remember where he'd left the rope and orange paint.

* * * *

Two hours later, Brad was frustrated.

May hadn't exactly been in a cooperative mood

once she figured out what he had in mind. He'd already tied her down, which kept her from going too crazy, but there was no way he could let her go now. Not until after Halloween. And by then, well, he doubted she'd been in a forgiving mood, given her current state.

He regarded her from his work stool as she sat tied to a folding chair across the room. The orange paint had stained her skin nicely - just a light wash was all it took. And the green he'd found had clumped nicely in large chunks of her hair to create a cascade of real-enough looking leaves. A bit of white for the triangles around her eyes and nose was cracking, but it was old paint, and before he'd found enough metal wire to create a stretcher frame for her lips, she'd moved around too much before the paint dried.

He'd touch that up later.

Now he just had to decide whether it was easier to store a live body or a corpse. The corpse would be safer, obviously, since it couldn't really run off (and if it did, well, that would be fitting for the season). A live body would need water and probably some sort of sustenance for the remaining three days...but no refrigeration, which was a plus, since he didn't own a large enough freezer.

Having no experience with corpses, he wasn't sure what kind of changes the body would go through either. And he was quite fond of how his little "Jill" had turned out so far. Those plump pumpkin-breasts were sure going to be a hit with the older teens and dads. The thought made him smile.

"So it's settled then," he said, enjoying the way her eyes darted nervously to him, and then around the room. They looked almost animalistic, wild when she did that. "I need you alive for the big show."

Perfectly freaky.

He'd have to make her somewhat comfortable though - she couldn't stay like that for four days. And he certainly wasn't going to clean up after her. Considering his options, he decided on the basement guest room and bathroom suite. No windows, thick concrete walls, a sturdy lock, and she'd be safe there until Halloween. His very own pumpkin-girl.

"I'm really glad you're staying, May. You'll be the star of the show, I promise. And when I win the Jack competition, we'll celebrate. How's that sound?"

Tears leaked from her eyes as she shook her head, trying to speak, but the wire holding her mouth in the standard toothy jack-o-lantern grimace wouldn't allow more than a strangled sound from her throat.

He walked over and untied her feet first, then cut the rope holding her arms to the chair while leaving her wrists bound. Slinging her over his shoulder, he took her to the house through the connecting door and deposited her on the bed in the basement guest room. Carefully removing the wire lip frame, he severed the rest of the ropes and left her sobbing on the old comforter his mother had made, locking the door behind him.

* * * *

The next morning Brad considered his options for Jill's breakfast. Finally settling on a protein shake, he mixed it up and put it in a water bottle with a tight lid. Sneaking down the stairs in stocking feet, he opened the door just enough to toss the bottle in. With it closed and locked again, he went upstairs to enjoy his own breakfast while drawing the new layout of his yard display to include one more.

It was going to be killer.

Smirking at his own joke, he refilled his coffee mug and went to the garage. Placing another practice pumpkin in the center of the table, he arranged his space as he had the day before and got to work, carving and drilling and shaping for hours until finally it was done.

Sitting back, he tilted his head one way and then the other to critique his work. It still wasn't quite right, but there wasn't too much more he could do with the sizing until he had all of the items needed. And the very last one wouldn't really be...available until the day of the contest.

Calling it a day, he went back inside and made another shake for Jill before making his own dinner. He'd just settled on the couch and turned on the TV when the phone rang.

"Hello Mom," he said into the receiver after glancing at the caller ID. "I was wondering if you'd call this week or not."

Her musical laugh in his ear made him smile. "Of course I did, darling. I know you're probably getting ready for the big contest on Friday. How are you doing with the pumpkin carving?"

He shrugged, muting the television sound. "I think I'm going to win this year, finally. I have this freaky idea for my Jack that's going to really scare the neighbors. And I decided to do a 'Jill' pumpkin too."

"That's wonderful, dear." His mother sighed. "I wish I could be there to see it, but I'm afraid I won't be back in the country just yet by then. Will you send me pictures?"

Brad nodded. "Sure Mom. Say, while I have you on the phone, I was thinking about taking a vacation when this is all over. Somewhere out of the country. Can you set something up for me? Somewhere warm?"

"Why I'd love to, dear! But why don't you just go stay in that house your father left you on that little island in the Caribbean? I can't remember the name of the island, but it's just sitting there empty, and you'd have the whole thing to yourself for as long as you want. Would that work?"

"You know, I'd forgotten all about that place. Thanks for the reminder! I'll send you pictures of the contest decorations when they're all outside. And I'll be on Dad's island for a month or two after that if you need me."

"Excellent, sweetheart. Maybe I'll even stop in for a visit while you're there. Let me know if you need anything, okay?"

"Will do. Thanks Mom. I've gotta go now, but I hope you have a Happy Halloween."

"Thank you, honey. And Happy Halloween to you too. Talk to you later, son."

He hung up the phone and grinned. He'd leave on Saturday for the private island his dad had left him in the will when he died three years ago. It would be the perfect place not only to hide out, but to dispose of a couple corpses. If he recalled correctly, the surrounding waters were infested with sharks that would make quick work of his clean-up job.

Raising the sound on the TV again, he settled in to watch for a bit before bed. Two more days until that trophy would finally be his.

* * * *

The next day Brad spent most of the day in his garage again with only a couple of quick breaks to mix up protein shakes for Jill. His grand collage was coming together and as soon as dusk fell, he began arranging the pumpkins he'd already carved with the various plastic skeletons, rats, bats and other spooky critters he'd collected over the years. Purple and orange lights were wound around and through trees to light the display, and strobe lights strategically placed to set off the empty spaces that waited for his main attractions.

Would they know, he wondered? Would they be able to tell real human flesh from polymer and plastic? Props had become so real-looking, television so violent that people often had a hard time distinguishing truth from fiction.

He was counting on it.

After one last look from the sidewalk to make sure everything was in place, he cut the lights and went inside to rest and relax. Tomorrow would be a very big day, and he'd need to be at the top of his game to pull the whole thing off.

Several hours later it was still dark outside when he woke to a loud thump outside his window, followed by quiet laughter. Thinking first of Jill, he ran down the stairs and listened at her door, but all was quiet.

Back upstairs, he went to the front door and peered out the window, his fingers curling to fists as he watched what looked to be a teenage boy hoist one of his jacks and send it sailing into the street where hours of his hard work exploded into thick fleshy pieces.

The kid wasn't alone - there were four that he could see. And judging by the stringy flesh all over the street, it wasn't just his jacks they were targeting.

His would be the last though.

Brad flung open the door and ran outside, making no sound as he launched himself at the kid on his lawn. They went down in a rough heap, the kid getting one strangled yelp out before Brad covered the small mouth with his hand. He looked up at the sound of footsteps fading to see the other boys disappear down the street. It was really too bad he could only take one, but an example had to be set.

"You think it's funny to ruin other people's property?" he asked, dragging the kid to his feet. "To throw away hours of sweat and planning and hard work?"

The boy shook his head, or tried, unable to move much in Brad's iron grasp. Brad raised his eyebrows. "No? Because that's what you just did tonight, son. And now I've got holes in my display that I'm afraid you're going to have to fill to make up for what you've done."

The kid seemed to relax a little as he glanced at the pumpkins in the street, and then the empty spaces on the lawn beside the driveway. He nodded against Brad's hand.

As if he had a choice.

Brad walked with him toward the garage and entered the code to open the door. Guiding the boy inside, he waited until the door was closed again before showing the kid to Jill's vacated seat.

"You just sit right here and we'll get to work replacing those pumpkins," he said, slowly moving his hand away from the kid's mouth.

"Yes sir," he said, his voice quiet. "I'm sorry Sir. I'll make you new ones. I won't do it again, I promise."

Brad smiled as he took some rope and a scarf off hooks on the wall. Luckily it was cooler out, and less than twenty-four hours until the contest started. No need to worry about accommodations for this one.

"I know you won't, kid. This is all gonna work out just fine."

* * * *

Brad woke up late the next day, bright mid-morning sun streaming through the sheers on his bedroom window. A glance at the clock told him he was already several hours behind.

"Fuck."

He sat up, head foggy and hurting from not enough sleep. The kid had taken far longer than he should have, and Brad had considered just staying up for the duration, but he'd finally laid down for a nap after slicing his arm with a sharp carving knife around six in the morning.

Extending his arm, he unwrapped the bloody gauze he'd hastily patched himself up with to check on the injury. The edges were clean, but separated to reveal the fatty layer underneath. He'd considered stitching it up but threading the needle had proven to be too much for his sleep-deprived fingers. He'd have to do it now, and hope that he could get through the rest of the day and night without pulling the stitches out.

Bypassing the beer in the refrigerator, he got the bottle of whiskey from a shelf in the living room and took it along with the supplies he'd need into the bathroom. Closing the door, he sat on the edge of the tub and hung his arm over it, fingers down. A long hiss escaped his lips as the liquor rushed over and through the wound, leaving behind an excruciating burn that made his whole body ache.

A little more whiskey in the bottom of the glass was deemed sufficient to sterilize the needle and thread. A long pull straight off the bottle burned down his throat, and he was ready to begin.

It took half an hour and several more shots to close the wound, and when he was done the bathtub was redder than the garage table had been after he'd finished with the kid. The stitches weren't pretty, but he flexed his fingers a few times to make sure they'd hold and then rinsed the whole thing with the rest of the bottle before wrapping it up with more gauze.

Turning on the sink faucet, he leaned over and stuck his head under the cold water, rinsing his hair with his good hand before shutting the water off and toweling it dry. It wasn't a shower, but close enough.

He had work to do, and it was time to get to work on his final and best piece for the contest tonight.

Dressing as quickly as he could, he went down to the kitchen and grabbed his keys, glancing at the blender as he walked past. Jill was just going to have to wait on her shake for a few more hours. There wasn't time to make one now, and it would be better to give her the last one on an empty stomach. The drugs would work better that way.

Out in the garage, he cleaned off the table and began setting up for the last project on his list. It would take an hour and twenty minutes to prepare the pumpkin, and then he could spend the rest of the afternoon finishing off the details. His display had to be complete no later than seven, so there was no room for error.

He moved the stool into position and got to work, calm and focused as he put drill to orange flesh. This was his year, his night to shine.

Time to show his neighbors just how badly he wanted that trophy.

* * * *

It was late afternoon when Brad finally walked down the street and asked Mason to come take a look at his display.

Mason took his ball cap off and ran his forearm across his sweaty brow. "I have my own stuff to put out, man. I'll come down a little later."

"I was kind of hoping to get your opinion though," Brad said, doing his best to sound humble. "You win every year, so obviously you're doing something right. I just thought you could help me out a bit, is all."

Mason was wavering. Brad could see it on his face, and it made him sick. People like Mason who looked down on everyone else just couldn't resist a chance to put another person in their place. Of course he'd come look. It would make him feel superior.

At least for the thirty seconds it took for the shot to kick in.

It wasn't long before Mason joined him in the garage. Brad drove the syringe into the thick muscle in Mason's neck, knowing there wasn't enough of the clear liquid to kill his prey. Brad wasn't even sure what it was called, or how it worked exactly, but a friend of a friend of a friend had assured him it would paralyze his props enough to keep them pliable, but not enough to stop their breathing.

Brad would do that himself afterward. The fear in their eyes was one of the most important pieces of the display.

It took longer than he'd thought to prepare Mason, but once the Jack mask was in place, Brad knew he'd made the right decision. It fit perfectly, the careful holes he'd made to reveal specific features proportioned just right. He wheeled the centerpiece out of his garage to the display area and situated him as he'd envisioned. Then he closed the garage door, triggered the lights, and stepped back to survey his work.

It was a gruesome scene, but tasteful. The practice Jacks shimmered out shadows with real candlelight - none of those fake safety lights for them. The Jack he'd made last night lay on his side, half covered in leaves with his bare torso streaked green and brown for a viney look. His hands were glued to the pumpkin encasing his head, as if he were trying to push it off. The pumpkin face was carved thin, but not all the way through, and it was only just possible to make out the human face behind the pumpkin flesh when the strobe flashed perfectly.

More leaves, more pumpkins, more practice Jacks arranged in a throne of sorts, where Jill sat perched in a long white skirt. Her upper body painted green as well, those lovely breasts bound to hold them upright in perfect globes were painted orange with brown accents and tips. Little tiny Jills, Brad thought with a smile. Her lips stretched wide and her was face painted in traditional jack-o-lantern form, her hair flowing neatly over her shoulders as her eyes darted eerily back and forth.

Next to her, Mason hung suspended from a thin wooden cross, straw hanging out of the denim legs of his well-worn overalls and the cuffs of a plaid flannel shirt. A ring of straw graced his neck too, just underneath the large Jack fitted around his head in two pieces and held together by leather straps and silver buckles. The grimace on his face formed the expression for the Jack, the anger and pain in his eyes giving the whole picture a far more horrifying look than even Brad had imagined when dreaming up the creation. Sure to scare anyone who dared look, and far better than anything Mason had ever put together.

A few adjustments to the strobe lights, and Brad was satisfied. He checked his watch - just ten minutes until the contest judges would be making their way down the street. Unwilling to leave the display now that it was up, he sat on the porch to wait, a beer in one hand, and a bucket of candy on the railing.

* * * *

Three hours, double as many beers and one bucket of candy later, Brad turned out the lights and began to move his largest props back into the garage. Calm on the outside, he was seething inside. A few people had loved the display - true aficionados, but the majority had shied away. What was wrong with people these days?

The Jack trophy had gone to a house two doors down and across the street. The yard was filled with those gaudy inflatable decorations, and the Jacks lining the walk weren't anything special. He was pretty sure the kids had done them; the cuts and shaping were so bad. When he'd gotten his contest score, the judges had all disqualified his display for being too scary for children, and too realistic.

What the hell?

He'd been pleasant about it, of course - he always was. But he'd realized at that moment that he'd never win the contest. They wouldn't let him. All these years, he'd thought it was judged objectively, but it wasn't, not really.

Briefly he entertained the idea of killing the judges, but he quickly discarded it. He wasn't a killer, not really. If there had been a way to keep the kid quiet...but he would have suffocated anyway. And he had smashed those pumpkins.

Still, he'd been uneasy with the whole thing, though he'd drowned out those thoughts with copious amounts of alcohol. And now that the adrenaline and motivation were gone, disposing of multiple bodies just seemed like...a lot of work.

He stood in the garage and looked at his Jack and Jill, heads hanging down and shoulders slumped after their long night out. They were still breathing, he knew, and it would certainly be easier to get them on the plane if they walked themselves.

Perhaps there was another way. They couldn't be allowed to live, obviously, but maybe he could arrange it so nature could simply take its course. No need for him to do the dirty work when plenty of other options were available.

Making sure their wrists and ankles were securely bound, Brad removed the Jack mask from Mason's head, and the bindings from May's breasts. Removing the spreader from her lips, he replaced it with a scarf tied behind her head, and fitted Mason with a similar one. Then he stepped back as both of them watched, wary and tense.

"Do you want to live?" he asked, figuring the best way to get them to cooperate was to give them hope. As expected, with some effort they both managed to nod.

"I thought so. We'll be leaving soon, and if you cooperate, everything is going to work out just fine. Understand?"

Two more nods.

Brad opened the door to the back yard and took the bag he'd packed earlier out to the car he'd parked in the alley. The kid was next, stashed in the trunk. He found a shirt to slip over May's head, so they didn't make too much of a scene at the airport, and then helped his 'guests' to the car.

Two hours later, they were settled in his private jet, cruising down a little-used runway and ready for takeoff. The pilot, having been with the family for years, was used to the sometimes dubious cargo he was paid well to carry without comment. Brad's parents had always had...interesting lives.

"I think you'll like the island," he said offhandedly

as he buckled in for departure. "I haven't been there in years, but I remember it's warm and isolated. A perfect place to retire."

Chuckling at the sudden panic in their eyes, he laid his seat back and closed his eyes, ready for a nice long nap.

* * * *

The sun was shining through the small window when Brad woke, and he smiled at the warmth on his face. Stretching his arms over his head, he yawned, and then turned to check on his 'guests'. Both had dozed off, and he watched long enough to make sure they were still breathing before making his way to the cockpit to check the flight status.

When he returned to his seat, two pairs of sleepy eyes regarded him warily. Seeing no need for the gags at this point, he cut them off.

"Water," Mason gasped out, with May nodding next to him. Brad shrugged. They weren't going to be alive much longer - the plane was preparing to land at the closest airport to his island, and then they'd transfer to his boat for the last leg of their trip. Once they docked, the reef sharks would get a nice meal, and the last evidence of his latest Halloween failure would be gone.

"I suppose it won't hurt." He opened two bottles of water and pushed a straw into the openings, holding them up for the captives to sip. When the bottles were empty, he buckled back into his seat as the plane began to descend.

It was mid-morning, and the airport was busy with tourists, but a private car with tinted windows met them at the door of Brad's plane and shuttled them directly to the dock. Once on board his private yacht, he laid the kid in back and tethered Mason and May to the metal railing where he could keep an eye on them and then took the wheel himself, piloting them out into the sparkling open water.

He felt better, the humid ocean breeze permeating his skin and filling his lungs with that smooth, salty-fresh scent. For miles around there was nothing but water, and he could just barely make out the island off in the distance, and he memories of a beach house on the far side flashed through his mind as he began to remember. Long, sunny days building sand castles and playing in the tide pools, warm nights with cool breezes and rhythmic waves singing him to sleep.

Then another, darker memory rose up in his mind, freezing him in place and setting his heart racing. There was a reason he'd never been back, and it all came flooding down over him in a fit of rage and anger. A dark night, cold water, and cruel hands holding him down in the sand as the tide tried to suck him out.

Drunken laughter as he tried not to swallow the

water. Struggled to get away. To breathe.

His mother knew. Knew what had happened, and knew he blocked it out. Yet she'd suggested this place, encouraged him to come.

She shouldn't have done that.

Brad started to turn the boat around, determined not to set foot on the island again. He'd find another place to vacation - the house in Monterrey, maybe. Then movement out the cockpit window caught his eye. May's skirt fluttered in the wind, her hair swirling around her head as she sat bound to the railing next to Mason. Their heads were bent together and they appeared to be talking quietly, though Brad couldn't hear a thing from behind the glass.

Damn it. For a few seconds he'd forgotten about them. Glancing up, he saw the island now closer than the mainland. He'd have to dump his cargo before he could go back - there was no other way.

He throttled back, letting the boat drift as he went to the storage locker just outside the cabin and checked on the supplies he'd had his assistants on the mainland ready before they boarded. Removing the padlock and pulling up the lid, he nodded in satisfaction. Six whole pumpkins, each with a rope threaded through the sides sat in a neat row ready for use.

Taking two out, he hauled them to the back of the boat and loosely secured them to the rail before he went back and got the boy's corpse. Tying one squash to each ankle, Brad took out a large fishing knife and made several cuts along the boy's limbs. The cuts didn't bleed so much as ooze, but it didn't matter. The sharks would smell it anyways, which was the point. Cleaning the knife in the water, he shoved the body off the back of the boat and watched it slowly sink into the depths.

Not willing to leave the clean-up to chance, Brad waited, watching the water. It wasn't long before a familiar triangle shape cut through the water as it came toward the yacht. He waited until at least three distinct fins had surfaced and disappeared before he staged the other four pumpkins at the back of the boat. Long, dark shapes swirled under and through the water, more by the minute.

Finally satisfied that there were enough scavengers below to complete his clean-up job, he went to get May.

"Ladies first!" he said, reaching for her bindings. She shook her head, trying to pull away thought there was nowhere for her to go.

"No! Please! You don't have to do this. I don't wanna die!" She cried and begged, her shoulder hitting him square in the stomach. He hauled back to punch the bitch, his need to get away from this place intensifying.

"Wait. Take me first."

Lowering his hand, Brad turned to Mason as May wept behind him. It didn't matter, he supposed. And maybe seeing Mason ripped apart would traumatize her into submission.

One could hope.

"Okay." He released Mason from the rail and led him to where he'd tethered the pumpkins. "Sit here, feet out."

Mason sat down, stretching his feet out and Brad began tying the rope of one squash to his ankle.

"Those are really nice," Mason said, eying the pumpkins. "They'd be good for carving. Can I see one? Sort of a last request?"

Brad frowned, rolling his eyes. "You're about to be eaten by sharks, and you want to carve a Jack?" Shaking his head, he placed one of the pumpkins in Mason's still bound hands. "Knock yourself out, but you've only got a minute or two. I need to get out of here, pronto."

Mason made a show out of examining the orange globe, his fingers gripping it tightly so it wouldn't fall. He looked at Brad still kneeling at his feet, and squinted against the sun.

"Thanks," he said, looking down at the pumpkin again. "But I had another idea." Bending his elbows, he thrust the pumpkin as hard as he could against Brad's face. The impact was jarring, and Brad felt his nose break as he lost his balance and toppled backward into the churning water.

Knowing he didn't have much time, Brad hoisted himself out of the water, feeling something huge below and hanging on tight to the railing as giant teeth clamped down on the tiny deck. The entire boat rocked back under the weight of the huge creature, and Brad kicked out at the blunt gray nose as it slid back into the water.

The pumpkins attached to Mason's feet rolled off the low dock with the pitching of the boat, and Mason scrabbled for a handhold as they pulled him along, briefly catching Brad's leg before slipping down into the depths. It wasn't long before the water boiled red, and Brad laughed in relief as he moved carefully to the higher part of the deck.

Breathing heavily, he quickly went to the wide-eyed woman and released her from the side railing. She didn't struggle as he led her to the back of the boat. Probably in shock from watching Mason's disposal. Pushing her down to the deck, he reached for one of the last two ropes, but she shook her head.

"Don't. I'll just...go." Her voice was calm, reasonable even, and he frowned in confusion.

"That doesn't make any sense. Why would you do that?"

She looked down at her chest then back up. Pointed to her face. "How could I ever go back like this? How could I ever live a normal life? You've ruined me. There's no point in living anymore."

He considered that for a moment. The logic was sound, he supposed, considering the extensive bruising where he'd bound her breasts and stretched her mouth. Those might heal, but the house paint on her skin was cracking too, and he noted more than a few spots where the flesh underneath seemed to be cracking along with it, leaving angry red, sometimes bloody welts showing through.

Nodding, he reached down to help her to her feet, and she stepped down onto the smaller dock. Dark gray fins circled anxiously, more than he'd expected. She stared at them for a long moment, and he moved in behind her, in case she needed one last bit of encouragement.

Turning, she smiled a sad smile. "Can I have just one last kiss? For old times?"

He shrugged and then leaned forward to press his lips softly against hers.

She wound her arms around his neck and kissed him back, then smiled as she toppled them both into the sea.

###

About the Author

Alex Westhaven resides in Billings, Montana with her husband and two over-sized lap dogs. Halloween is her favorite holiday, and she has more than her fair share of skeletons (and other body parts) in the closet. Stop by AlexWesthaven.com for all the latest horror news and upcoming books.